CAT TAILS

Herta Rousseau

ISBN: 978-1-63684-607-1   (Paperback Edition)
ISBN: 978-1-63684-608-8   (Hardcover Edition)
ISBN: 978-1-63684-606-4   (E-book Edition)

Some characters and events in this book are fictitious. Any similarity to real persons, living or dead, is coincidental and not intended by the author.

Book Ordering Information

Phone Number: 315 288-7939 ext. 1000 or 347-901-4920
Email: info@globalsummithouse.com
Global Summit House
www.globalsummithouse.com

Printed in the United States of America

I would like to dedicate these pages to all my fellow cat lovers and to the numerous animal advocates everywhere working to make better lives for our furry friends.

INTRODUCTION

When my children grew up we always had some kind of a pet. They were considered family and naturally the kids attributed certain feats to the animal. Any kind of news or happening of the day was always connected to or with the animal. Later, when only my youngest daughter was still living at home there came this, "Mushroom Period." Lots of items sold and available had mushrooms and I joined in and painted them. From there we transferred the sayings of the animals to the mushrooms; we made little comic strips for ourselves. Then other things took over and the files were put aside.

After discovering some of these long ago sketches when I moved to California a thought occurred to transfer these to my cat family who meanwhile had adopted me. Always being concerned with animals before, it was easier at this point to take care of cats. I had no thought of printing the book until several people suggested it. Here's hoping that this reader too will like it and maybe get a laugh or two out of it and it might remind people of the numerous cats and dogs without homes that are in need of someone to love them. My heart goes out to them and I wished I could save them all.

and its housekeeping staff

reside here

Eating and Drinking is dangerous to your health

Everyone needs a little T.L.C.
"Tender Loving Cat"

It's nice to have a friend to do
absolutely nothing with

Hey, this is my coffee!

"Great place to have lunch,
just don't open the door"

Not tonight I have a haddock

I got you a spare Lap for kitty
you put him on it whenever you are busy

Cattet

Charlie, just how much Cat-Nip
has fluffy been taking?!!

and I was afraid the cat door would not work

I've abandoned my search for truth and
now I'm looking for a good fantasy

I know it all, I just can't remember it all at once

Sometimes it's nice to stay undercover.

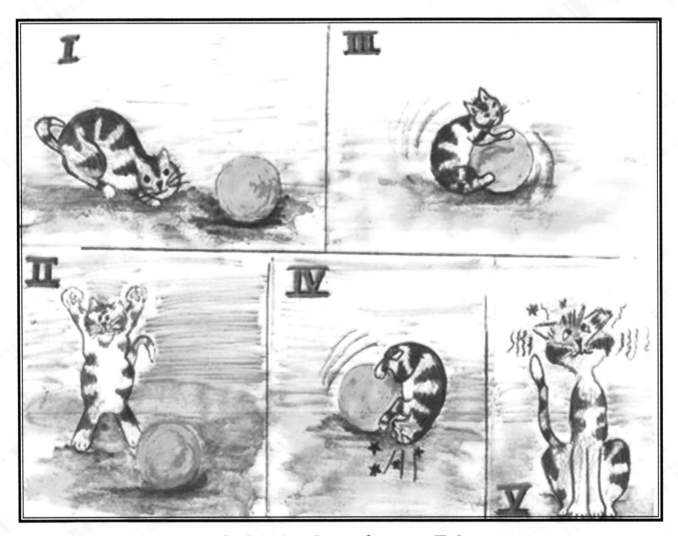

It looked easier on TV

This is the best present ever.
I always wanted one like this

Women like
the simple things
in life:
men

When you said you wanted a big family I had
no idea this is what you meant

When the owners are away ...

... And when they're at home ...

Do you have anything larger than a king size?

Concert under the stars

**Do you get the feeling lately that
something has come between us?**

Skinny dipping for Cats

I talk to her because she listens

See no evil, hear no evil, speak no evil

... but he's keeping my feet warm ...

"Here's your order"

Strip Poker

"Are you getting off the furniture or do I have to get the vacuum cleaner?"

New Event at the Olympics:
"Cat bath"

Mardi Paws

When the owners are asleep ...

**GOLF ISN'T A RICH MAN'S GAME:
THERE ARE MILLIONS OF POOR PLAYERS**

Hypnotize me? Never!

"I have to make different seating arrangements around here ..."

"There is no code to break,
it's Alphabet Soup"

**All things considered,
Insanity is the only alternative.**

"It's a cats world. I'm just here to open cans."

"See, here's the invoice.
It proves I paid for this bed."

PRESERVE WILD LIFE
... THROW A PARTY

Some people own cats and lead normal lives

Nine computer challenged lives

Computeritis

Follow your Bliss

What else can one ask for if you have the most beautiful cat in the world?

I'll have tuna please

Second Hand Smoke

**AN OBJECT AT REST TENDS TO REMAIN AT REST
BY: SIR ISAAC NEWTON**